Vlad the Drac

Vlad the Drac the tiny vegetarian vampire has been invited to London to attend the first night of a new film: *The Wickedest Vampire in the World.* Now that Vlad is no longer a secret he doesn't want to stay with his old friends, the Stone family, no he wants to be a guest at the best hotel in town. Unfortunately, the other guests have different ideas!

As ever, Vlad can't stay out of trouble for long and he falls foul of the Hoover, the food mixer and Mr Punch during his stay in England.

A hilarious sequel to *Vlad the Drac.*

Other Books by Ann Jungman

Vlad the Drac · *Barn Owl Books*

Bold Bad Ben the Beastly Bandit · *Barn Owl Books*

Clottus and the Ghostly Gladiator · *A & C Black*

Bacillus and the Beastly Bath · *A & C Black*

Twitta and the Ferocious Fever · *A & C Black*

Tertius and the Horrible Hunt · *A & C Black*

Over the Rainbow · *Oxford University Press*

Resistance! · *Barrington Stoke*

Ann Jungman

VLAD THE DRAC RETURNS

ILLUSTRATED BY GEORGE THOMPSON

BARN OWL BOOKS

Originally published by Dragon Books in 1984
This edition published in 2004 by Barn Owl Books
157 Fortis Green Road, London N10 3LX
Barn Owl Books are distributed by Frances Lincoln
4 Torriano Mews, Torriano Avenue, London NW5 2RZ

ISBN 1 903015-34-0

Designed and typeset by Douglas Martin Associates, Oadby
Printed and bound in Great Britain by
Creative Print & Design Wales, Ebbw Vale

Contents

1 Vlad Returns 9

2 A Chapter of Disasters 19

3 Vlad Goes to School 32

4 Vlad Goes Swimming 44

5 Vlad's Concert 57

6 Vlad's Journey 71

7 A Day by the Sea 80

8 The Vampire's Revenge 91

9 Vladnapped 99

10 Vlad Makes Good 111

For Allan

I

Vlad Returns

'Judy!' called her mother. 'Come and have breakfast. There's a letter for you from Romania.'

Judy rushed downstairs followed by Paul. 'Where's my letter, Mum?'

'There by your plate,' replied Mrs Stone. 'Is it from Vlad?'

'Must be,' said Judy, tearing the envelope open. 'But it's not like him to write letters, I hope everything is alright.'

'Come on,' said Paul, 'read it out, what does it say?'

So Judy read: 'Dear Judy and Paul and Mum and Dad. Guess what! I'm coming to England. Some people have made a film called *The Wickedest Vampire in the World.* I suppose it's about Great Uncle Ghitza. Anyway I've been asked to attend the first night and so I will be arriving in London on May 4th. The first night isn't till the end of May but I want to spend sometime in London. I have a fan club now (I call it my fang club). They are making all the arrangements for my stay. As I am now very important, I will be staying at a big hotel. I expect I'll be very busy but if I do have any time I'll try and give you a ring and maybe if you're lucky we can meet for tea. Hope this finds you well as it leaves me, – Vlad.'

'Well,' said Paul, 'how about that! Vlad's coming to London and doesn't think he'll have time to see us!'

'How can he be so horrid, Mum?' asked Judy, almost in tears. 'We were the first people Vlad ever knew and he doesn't even want to see us.'

'I wouldn't get too upset about it if I were you,' said Mrs Stone. 'Something tells me we'll be hearing from Vlad very soon.'

'I'd be willing to take a bet on it,' said Mr Stone.

'When is the 4th of May anyway?' asked Paul.

'It's today,' said Mr Stone, looking at his watch.

'Oh Dad! Can we go to the airport to meet Vlad?' asked Judy. 'Please, oh please!'

'No, you can't,' said her father. 'We don't know which flight he's coming on and you've got to go to school anyway.'

So the children went off to school but spent most of the day wondering if Vlad had arrived and what would happen when he did. Judy slumped down in front of the television feeling very fed up when at last she got home. Then suddenly she sat bolt upright.

'And after the news headlines,' said the announcer, ' we will have a very unusual item. In the studio we have the pint-sized vegetarian vampire, Vlad the Drac, who has just flown in from Romania.'

'Mum, Dad, Paul!' yelled Judy. 'Come quick! Vlad's on the telly.'

The Stones gathered round the television.

'Good evening, Vlad,' said the announcer. 'Am I right in thinking that you're one of the last vampires in the world?'

'Well,' said Vlad, who was sitting on the arm of the announcer's chair, 'I thought I was the last of the vampires, but then I met Mrs Vlad and now we have five children, so we're on the increase.'

'Well, that is good news,' said the announcer.

'I wouldn't be too sure of that,' said Vlad. 'I'm pleased, naturally, being a vampire, but if I was a person I might be worried. I mean I'm harmless. I'm a vegetarian. But my son Ghitza . . . Now he's a very naughty little vampire, and not a vegetarian, I can tell you!'

'Oh dear,' said the announcer. 'Now can you tell us why you're in London?'

'I'm here to atend the first night of a film about my Great Uncle Ghitza and I'm also on a goodwill mission to improve relations between vampires and people.'

'Let me wish you the best of luck in that, Vlad the Drac, it's been a pleasure to have you in the studio and we hope to see you again.'

'Thank you,' said Vlad, and pretended to vampirize the announcer's ear.

The Stones stared at the screen in amazement.

'Vlad always wanted to be a star, and now he's made it,' said Paul.

'Vlad on TV,' said Judy. 'I can hardly believe it. He must be very important. No wonder he doesn't want to see us.'

'You wait and see,' commented Mum, '*You* just wait and see.

Late that night the children were asleep and their parents were getting ready for bed when the phone rang.

'Who can it be at this hour?' moaned Dad from the shower.

'I'll take it,' called Mum, wiping the toothpaste off her mouth as she ran to the phone. 'Hello, Catherine Stone speaking,' she said, picking up the receiver.

Paul and Judy were now at their bedroom doors to hear what was going on.

'Yes, yes,' they heard Mum say. 'This *is* Dr Stone.' There was a pause. 'Oh,' she said. 'Oh dear, yes, I see the problem.'

'Who is it?' shouted Dad from the bathroom.

'It's the manager of the Ritz Hotel. It seems that Vlad's in a bit of trouble.'

Dad and Judy and Paul all came running and stood in a huddle around the telephone.

'Yes, I see,' said Mum. 'Oh, how awful. Yes, yes, we'll come and fetch him as soon as possible. Thank you. Goodbye.'

'Is poor little Vlad alright?' said Judy anxiously.

'What's he been up to now?' demanded Paul.

'We'd better all get dressed,' said their mother. 'There was some kind of problem in the dining room of the hotel and the manager was very, very upset and wants Vlad to leave immediately.'

'But why did they phone *us*?' asked Dad.

'Vlad gave us as his next of kin,' explained Mum.

'Oh,' said Dad in a surprised tone. 'I'm not sure I want to be next of kin to a vampire. Still, we'd better hurry and fetch him, I suppose.'

'Wait for us!' yelled the children rushing to grab their clothes.

So five minutes later the Stones were in their car heading for central London. They parked outside the hotel and went in. Judy looked round at the huge lobby, the thick red carpets and the crystal chandeliers.

'It's very grand, isn't it?' she whispered. 'Fancy Vlad being able to afford to stay here.'

A worried looking man came up to the Stones.

'Are you Mr Stone?' he asked.

'Yes,' said Dad, and shook hands with the man. 'We came as soon as we got your call. What's the problem?'

The man wiped his brow and heaved a sigh of relief. 'Thank goodness you're here. We've been having such a time of it.'

'Whatever has Vlad done?' asked Judy.

'Oh nothing,' the hotel manager assured her. 'It's not him at all. It's the other guests, they seem to feel a bit insecure with a vampire under the same roof.'

'But he's not at all vampirish,' protested Judy. 'Is he, Mum?'

'Of course he's not,' Mum agreed. 'He's a friendly little fellow.'

'I know, I know,' said the manager, 'but I couldn't convince the other guests of that. They said he had to go or else they would, so I had no choice but to phone you and ask you to take him away.'

'But that's not fair,' said Paul indignantly. 'Poor old Vlad!'

'That's just what *he* keeps saying,' said the manager.

'Oh yes,' Mum smiled. 'Poor old Vlad, poor little Drac.'

'Exactly.'

'Same old Vlad,' chorused the children.

'We left him in one of the offices with a member of staff,' said the manager. 'It seemed safer. Follow me, please.'

They trooped off through the splendid foyer, along a corridor and into a small room. There was Vlad, sitting on a desk talking to an off-duty receptionist. He was so busy talking that he didn't notice the Stones at first.

'Yes,' he was saying, 'Great Uncle Ghitza visited the first hotel the people built in Romania and he vampirised every single guest in one night. That was done as a warning to any future tourists, and then . . .' Vlad suddenly spotted the Stones. 'Oh there you are, I've decided to stay with you instead.'

Mum caught the children's eyes. 'That is very nice of you, Vlad,' she said.

'Jolly well is,' agreed Vlad. 'Let's go.'

'If you wouldn't mind using the back door,' said the hotel manager, stifling an embarrassed cough. 'It might be easier.'

'Why should we sneak out the back way?' demanded Dad. 'None of us has done anything wrong.'

'Yes,' agreed Mum. 'We'll go out the front entrance, thank you, just as we came in.'

So the family marched through the hotel and out of the swing doors into the street. Judy put Vlad on the roof of the car so that she could climb in. Then they heard a voice.

'There he is, there's the vampire!'

The Stones looked up and saw the hotel guests leaning out of their bedroom windows.

'Go on, you go away!' yelled one.

'Vampires out!' shouted another.

The cry of 'Vampires out!' was taken up. 'Vampires out! Vampires out!' they chanted.

Vlad shook his fist at them. 'You moth-eaten, no good bunch of mangleworzels,' he yelled back.' You knock-kneed mangy gang of . . .'

'Get Vlad in the car, quickly!' said Dad, revving up the engine. 'Let's get away from here.'

Judy grabbed Vlad, who was leaping up and down with rage. The car took off. The guests cheered. Vlad wriggled loose from Judy's arms and, leaning out of the window, shrieked:

'I'll tell my son Ghitza about you, you lousy bunch of . . .'

Fortunately at this point Judy grabbed Vlad and closed the window.

The vampire sat on Judy's knee, flushed and subdued. Gradually his face crumpled and he burst into tears.'Whatever's the matter, Vlad?' asked Judy, bending over him.

'Those people in the hotel,' sobbed Vlad. 'They didn't like me.' And he began to howl inconsolably.

'But what happened, Vlad?' asked Judy. 'Would you like to tell us all about it?'

'Nothing to tell,' sniffed the vampire. 'I went down to supper in my dinner suit. I'd booked a table. I sat down and bowed to the gentlemen and smiled at the ladies – and they all rushed out and made such a fuss.'

Vlad sniffed and Judy gave him a tissue.

He sniffled into it all the way home.

The vampire was still very upset and tearful when they drew up outside the Stones' house.

'I want to go back to Romania,' he wailed. 'People don't like me here, and I don't like people.'

'We'll talk about it in the morning, Vlad,' said Mum. 'You go up with Judy and you can sleep in your old drawer.'

'Yes,' soothed Judy, 'I can make it nice. I'll put all my socks in a nest for you. You'll like that.'

'No, I won't,' said Vlad. 'I don't want to sleep next to your smelly old socks.' But he went upstairs with

Judy and got into the drawer anyway.

'You won't turn the light out, will you?'

'No, Vlad,' replied Judy, kissing him goodnight. 'And if you wake up, I'm just over there in my bed.'

Vlad sniffed. 'I don't like people, Judy. You won't become a person when you grow up, will you?'

'I think I probably will,' said Judy apologetically.

'Then you'll get vampirized, like all the rest!'

'You wouldn't vampirize *me*,' laughed Judy.

'I wouldn't count on that,' said Vlad. 'I've got contacts, I've got connections. I could make arrangements. Now, close the drawer so there's only a little light. That's right. Night, Judy.' And within minutes Vlad was sleeping peacefully in his old drawer.

2

A Chapter of Disasters

The next morning Mrs Stone crept into Judy's bedroom.

'How's Vlad?' she whispered.

'He's still asleep,' said Judy. 'He went off straight away and hasn't woken up yet.'

'Yes I have,' called Vlad. 'Morning, all.'

'Hello, Vlad,' said Mum. 'Nice to see you, come and have some breakfast. I've got some nice washing-up liquid all ready – your favourite kind.'

'Good,' said Vlad. 'That's what I like for my breakfast.'

'And what do you like for other meals?' asked Mum. 'I'm not sure how much of a vegetarian you are.'

'I don't eat meat and I don't like blood,' explained Vlad, pulling a face. 'Ugg – blood! Horrible!'

'Most vegetarians like to eat beans,' suggested Mum.

'Beans!' said Vlad, livening up and giggling. 'Yeh, human beins!'

'No; seriously Vlad,' laughed Mum. 'What do you like to eat?'

'Well,' said Vlad. 'Let's see – I like washing-up liquid, soap, scouring powder, floor polish, shoe polish, window cleaning fluid, furniture . . .'

'Alright, alright,' said Dad. 'You don't have to list them all, we get the idea.'

Vlad picked up his washing-up liquid and beamed as he sat at the table with the rest of the family.

'I like this,' he said. 'In the old days, when I stopped with you before, I used to have to hang about upstairs while you all had your meals down here. This is much better.'

'So you think you'll stay in England, after all?' asked Dad.

'No,' moaned Vlad dramatically. 'People don't like me. I want to go home, where I know I'm wanted.'

'Oh, dear,' said Dad. 'You see, I've been talking to the secretary of your fan club and they say you must stay for the first night because the film company paid your fare to come here.'

Vlad's eyes began to fill up with tears. 'I want to go home!' he howled.

Just then the morning paper flopped through the letter box and Paul went to fetch it. A moment later he was back in the kitchen, shouting excitedly.

'Look, just look at this, look Vlad, you're on the front page!'

Vlad flew over and sat on the boy's shoulder.

'It's my picture,' he yelled. 'Whoopee!'

'What does it say?' asked Mum.

'Read it, read it, someone,' squeaked Vlad, leaping up and down with excitement.

'Vlad the Drac, the vegetarian vampire who has been delighting tourists by flying round Count Dracula's castle with his family in Romania, is visiting Britain. Vlad revealed that he had previously lived in London with a family who found him while they were in Romania on holiday. The vampire assured everyone that his visit was to improve relations between vampires and people. This paper would like to add its voice to all those that have welcomed Vlad to this country and wish him the best of luck with his mission.'

'Well,' said Vlad, glowing with pride. 'So all the people aren't like those ones in the hotel.'

'They didn't know about you,' explained Dad. 'Now everyone will realize you're harmless and they won't be frightened any more.'

'You're famous, Vlad,' said Judy. 'Maybe you won't want to stay at our house after all.'

'Yes, I do,' he assured her. 'I don't trust people, I'd rather be here with my friends.' And he swooped twice around the breakfast table to show he meant it.

'Time for school, children,' reminded Dad, ducking slightly. 'Come on, grab your things, I'll run you there.'

'Come on, Judy,' said Paul. 'I can't wait to tell the other kids that Vlad's staying with us.'

Vlad and Mum went to wave goodbye as the others drove off.

'I'll look after Vlad,' Mum called, 'so don't worry. I'm not going to work and we'll have a lovely day.'

When the children got home from school, however, they found Vlad sitting on the fridge with a sulky expression on his face and his back to their mother.

'Oh, there you are, at last,' he said. 'About time, too. Not a thought for me stuck at home all day. Poor old Vlad, poor little Drac.'

'But you've been with Mum all day,' said Paul. 'We thought you'd enjoy that.'

'Yes,' said Vlad, 'well I thought so, too. But we were all wrong, it's been the worst day of my life.'

'The worst day of *your* life,' said Mum indignantly. 'I feel as though I've been pulverized, it's been one disaster after another.'

'I'll make you a cup of tea,' said Judy. 'You look as though you need it.'

'That's right,' grumbled Vlad. 'Think about her. Not a word for me.'

'Sorry, Vlad,' said Judy soothingly. 'I'll get you some washing-up liquid, shall I?'

'No point,' sniffed Vlad. 'On top of everything else, that woman has just done the washing with my supper.'

'Oh,' said Judy. 'But never mind, I expect there's a spare in the cupboard.'

'No there isn't,' said Vlad gloomily. 'She's used up the last one.'

'And whose fault is that?' snapped Mum. 'If you hadn't gone mad in the supermarket I'd have been able to buy a spare bottle.'

'What happened in the supermarket, then?' asked Paul nervously.

'I was only trying to help,' protested Vlad. 'We were walking round the shop and I saw this huge pile of washing-up liquid. Naturally I wanted Mum to buy the most delicious one, so I pulled a bottle out from the bottom of the pile, just to have a taste, and . . .'

'Oh, I see,' said Paul. 'So the whole pile fell on top of you. And then what?'

'Well,' said Vlad. 'Imagine the scene. There was I, surrounded by all these bottles, so naturally I had to have a taste of all of them.'

'Oh dear,' sighed Judy faintly. 'Were the shop very angry?'

'Well actually, no,' said Vlad. '*She* was' (pointing at Mum) 'but then a surprising thing happened. A lady who was shopping asked the manager of the shop if she could buy one of the vampirized bottles as a souvenir of Vlad the Drac for her daughter. Soon everyone in the supermarket wanted one and the shopkeeper charged more for them than if they'd been full. So it was all right in the end.'

'And that's why there's no more washing-up liquid for Vlad to drink,' said Mum. 'He vampirized them all and now he's complaining that he's got no supper.'

'Food is the last comfort left to me,' moaned Vlad, 'and now I am deprived even of that. Poor old Vlad, poor little Drac.'

'What else happened?' asked Judy.

'You may well ask,' declared Vlad. 'What *didn't* happen, more like.'

'Well, are you going to tell us about it or are you not?' demanded Paul.

'I most certainly am,' said Vlad. 'I, in the course of today, have been boiled, whipped, minced, liquidized and hoovered.'

BRA
NEW
SUP

'What on earth are you talking about?' asked Judy, puzzled.

'It all began,' said Vlad, 'when Mum decided to make a shepherd's pie.'

'What's wrong with that?'

'First of all she boiled the potatoes, and as I stood on the edge of the saucepan to check that it was boiling I fell in and got boiled.'

'It was only for a second,' protested Mum. 'I fished you out as soon as I realized.'

'Only for a second!' exclaimed Vlad, outraged. 'It was quite long enough, let me tell you. And then she decided to whip the potatoes in that horrible mixing machine, and I just wanted to see what was going on and I fell in and got whipped.'

'I switched off the mixer the moment I noticed,' said Mum defensively.

'And then,' Vlad went on grimly, 'she decided to mince the meat.'

'Yes,' groaned Mum, 'and Vlad got too close again and fell in.'

'I was within an inch of getting minced too,' he said.

'Oh dear,' Judy murmured, trying not to laugh. 'You have had a day!'

'And you haven't heard the half of it yet,' Vlad

continued. 'As if she hadn't done enough damage, she then decided to liquidize some apples, for pudding.'

'I did warn you to stay well clear of the liquidizer,' snapped Mum.

'Yes, but I was trying to help, I just wanted to make sure the apples were smooth . . .'

'. . . but you fell in,' said Paul.

'Well yes,' admitted Vlad. 'In my anxiety to be helpful, I tipped over.'

'What a chapter of disasters,' said Judy. 'You have had an awful day, Vlad.'

'And I haven't got to the end yet,' said the vampire. 'After that Mum decided to clean the upstairs, and I went with her so she wouldn't get lonely and feel sad . . . and she hoovered me.'

'What do you mean?' asked Paul.

'You know, *hoovered*! I got sucked into that horrible noisy thing that she uses to clean the carpets.'

'Well why didn't you stay away from the hoover?' asked Judy. 'Mum must have told you to.'

'Well, she did,' admitted Vlad, 'but I was just checking that everything was working right, when pfft! – I was sucked up and sent whirling round and round in a sea of dust. It's still making me cough!' And Vlad proceeded to cough magnificently.

'Give him a drink, there's plenty of cold drinks in the fridge,' said Mum.

Paul opened the fridge and peered in. He took out some cans of orange and he and Judy sat down to drink theirs.

'How was your day at school?' asked their mother. 'Tell me about it quick, before Vlad starts complaining again.'

'Where *is* Vlad?' asked Judy. 'He was on the fridge a moment ago when we got our drinks out.'

They stared at each other in silent horror. They could hear a muffled knocking and small shouts of 'Let me out, I'm freezing to death!'

'I think we've shut him in the fridge!' Paul rushed over to open the door. Inside was Vlad, enclosed in a block of ice.

'Oh dear,' said Judy, giggling. 'Look at that! One deep frozen vampire! Poor old Vlad!'

'Here,' said Mum. 'Put him in this bowl of warm water to defrost.'

After a little while Vlad melted and climbed indignantly out of the bowl on to the drainingboard.

'This is the end,' he announced. 'Absolutely the end. Now I've been boiled, whipped, minced, liquidized, hoovered *and* deep frozen. I hate kitchens! I want to go home.'

'But why did you climb into the fridge?'

'I was only . . .'

'. . . trying to help,' chorused the family.

'Exactly! And as for that other horrible thing,' said Vlad, staring balefully at the mixer, 'I hate it, it's a twentieth century instrument of torture – there ought to be a law against them. I mean, at least the telephone that murdered Great Uncle Ghitza had the good manners to kill him outright. It didn't slowly torture him to death.'

'I'm very sorry, Vlad, but I did keep warning you to stay out of the way,' said Mum.

'But I only wanted to help.'

The Stones groaned.

'And what is more,' continued Vlad, undeterred, 'I don't see why you need that horrible thing, anyway. When my old grannie Natalia used to prepare a vampire feast, she only used a knife and a chopping board. None of this fancy stuff for my old grannie.'

'Well I don't suppose your old grannie had a job like I have,' snapped Mum.

'Not have a job!' exclaimed the outraged Vlad. 'My grannie Natalia was a full-time vampire, I'll have you know. She worked the night shift. Grandma Natalia was Great Uncle Ghitza's sister, and if he was afraid of anyone it was her. Yes, and even when she was very old she could cook a meal without one of those machines.'

'What did she cook, this famous grannie of yours?' asked Paul.

'People,' said Vlad. 'She did a lovely curry, did my grannie.'

'Uggh,' said Judy.

'I think you're making all of this up,' said Paul.

Vlad grinned. 'Only the bit about the curry. All the rest is true.'

'Vlad,' said Mum, 'I want you to promise me two things. First of all, never go near the mixer again.'

'Agreed,' said Vlad. 'And?'

'And never, never try to help again.'

'All right,' groaned Vlad. 'Bit I don't know what I'm supposed to do with myself every day.'

'You can come to school with us,' said Judy. 'When the kids at school heard that you were here they were all very excited and wanted to send you cards. The head teacher says you can come to school with us tomorrow if you like.'

'Cards,' said Vlad, brightening up. 'Cards for me, where, show me!'

So Judy got out a whole bag full of cards from the children at the school, all wishing Vlad luck and begging him to come and pretend to vampirize them. Vlad was delighted.

'Of course I'll come,' he said. 'I always did want to be a children's vampire. This is the beginning of my career as a vampire who specializes in children.'

3

Vlad Goes to School

It was Vlad's day to go to school. When Judy woke up she was surprised to hear him chattering away at the top of his voice. She opened her eyes and sat up. There was Vlad standing on the window sill carrying on an animated conversation.

'Oh Vlad, it's very early, what on earth are you doing?'

'I'm chatting up the birds,' replied Vlad. 'What else is there for a vampire to do? All people want to do is sleep.'

'Alright,' sighed Judy, 'I'll get up.'

'Can I hide in your duffle bag?' asked Vlad. 'I want to go into school secretly and give all the children a surprise in assembly.'

So after breakfast Vlad climbed into the bag and he, Judy and Paul left for school. As soon as they arrived the two children took Vlad to meet Mrs Thompson, their head teacher.

'Where's Vlad?' she asked, looking around.

'I'm in here,' called Vlad from the bag. 'Let me out!'

Judy opened the bag and out Vlad flew.

'Vlad,' said Judy, 'this is Mrs Thompson. She's the head of our school.'

'How do you do, madam,' said Vlad, holding out his hand. 'You're not the lady teacher I vampirized last time I visited this school, are you?'

'No,' said Mrs Thompson, smiling. 'We're so glad that you liked the cards the children sent you and could come and see us.'

'It was so nice to get them,' Vlad told her. 'I was quite depressed, and then suddenly there were all those nice cards from all the nice children.'

'The children are waiting for you in the hall now,' said Mrs Thompson. 'Are you ready?' So Vlad went into assembly sitting on Mrs Thompson's shoulder.

As they came in all the children were sitting in rows on the floor, and when they saw Vlad they cheered and whistled. Vlad bowed and waved in return. Mrs Thompson sat down and asked the children to be quiet.

'Good morning, children,' she said when they had finally settled down. 'Today we're very lucky because we must be the only school in Britain, and probably in the whole world, to have a vampire come and visit us. On behalf of the school I want to welcome you, Vlad.'

The children all clapped enthusiastically.

'Now Vlad, I wonder if you would mind telling us about your life in Romania.'

'It will be a pleasure,' said Vlad. And he stood on the table and told the children all about his ravine and Count Dracula's castle and Mrs Vlad and their five children.

The children listened eagerly to every word. You could have heard a pin drop. Then when he had finished Vlad asked if he could sing his vampire song and if the children could join in. And he sang:

'Blood, blood glorious blood,
Nothing quite like it for mixing with mud.
So follow me, follow,
Down my mouth's hollow,
And there let us wallow in glorious blood.'

After they'd sung the song three times right through, Mrs Thompson asked if anyone wanted to ask Vlad a question. A forest of hands shot up. One little girl clambered to her feet.

'Could you show us how you fly round the castle?' she asked.

'May I?' asked Vlad.

Mrs Thompson nodded. So Vlad flew round the room, twisting and turning like an aeroplane at a display and deafening everyone by trying to imitate an engine. Eventually he landed on the table.

'We do it twice a day for the tourists,' he explained. 'It's much better when there are seven of us. I first learned to fly when I was staying at Judy and Paul's. I used to use their dad's piano as a musical runway when I practised. Like this' he shouted and flew over to the piano. 'Like this!' he yelled.

Mrs Thompson tried to close the piano lid but she was too late.

'Shall I do it again? he asked.

'Yes!' chorused the children.

'No,' said Mrs Thompson. 'Any more questions?'

A boy stood up. 'Do your children go to school?' he asked.

'Not yet,' said Vlad.

'Lucky things,' said the boy. 'How can I become a vampire? I'd like just flying round a castle all day scaring people.'

'Can you tell us something about your Great Uncle Ghitza?' asked another child.

'Tell you about Great Uncle Ghitza,' said Vlad enthusiastically. 'I most certainly can! He wasn't a bit like me, he was a very vampirish vampire. Whenever he saw a human being, either sex, any age, his policy was: vampirize 'em! So he'd sniff a person, like this,' (Vlad flew round the room, sniffing) 'then he'd fix his steely gaze on his victim, open his huge mouth and snarl to show his massive fangs, and within a second his victim would be vampirized – like this!' And suddenly – Vlad flew back on to Mrs Thompson's shoulder and pretended to sink his fangs into her neck.

Mrs Thompson decided that all this was going

on too long.

'Alright children,' she said. 'Assembly is over now. Vlad will come and visit you in your classrooms a bit later. On behalf of the whole school, Vlad, may I thank you for giving up your valuable time and coming to see us here. Three cheers for Vlad.'

'No, not three,' shouted Vlad. 'Fifty-three.'

'Why fifty-three?' asked a surprised Mrs Thompson.

'Vampires always have fifty-three cheers,' Vlad explained. 'When Great Uncle Ghitza didn't get fifty-three cheers, there was some terrible vampirizing done that night, I can tell you.'

'Well Great Uncle Ghitza isn't here, thank goodness,' said Mrs Thompson, 'so three cheers for Vlad. Hip, hip, hip . . .' and all the children yelled 'Hooray' as hard as they could.

Vlad was delighted and asked if he could play the piano as the children went out of assembly. So the children filed out of assembly calling 'Goodbye Vlad' while he ran up and down the piano calling back 'See you soon.'

When the children had gone Vlad hopped on to Mrs Thompson's shoulder and they went back into her room.

'That was very nice,' said the vampire. 'Those

children really liked me. You know, I really like children, it's people I don't like. Well, most people anyway. You're alright.'

'Maybe it's because I spend so much time with children,' suggested Mrs Thompson.

'Yes,' agreed Vlad. 'I think that's what it must be.'

When Paul went to Mrs Thompson's room to fetch Vlad he was nowhere to be seen, but Paul noticed a strange muffled sound coming from the cupboard.

'You told me to come and fetch Vlad at ten-thirty, Mrs Thompson,' said Paul.

'Yes,' said Mrs Thompson. 'You can take him in a minute. He's in that cupboard having fifty-three cheers for himself. He agreed to do it in the cupboard so that I could get on with some work. He'll knock when he's finished.'

'Thank you for letting us bring him to school,' said Paul. 'Vlad was getting very miserable and homesick and anti-people – coming to school and everyone being so pleased to see him has really cheered him up.'

A minute later Vlad knocked and Mrs Thompson let him out of the cupboard.

'I'm thirsty,' he announced.

'I'm not surprised,' said Mrs Thompson. 'Well,

I'm going to have a cup of tea and the children drink milk. Do either of those tempt you?'

'Ugg no,' said Vlad pulling a face. 'Horrid!'

'I'll ask the cook what she's got in the kitchen, then,' said Mrs Thompson.

'I think we'd be better to ask the school keeper,' said Paul. 'Vlad has very odd tastes.'

So some oil that was used on creaking doors and rusty bicycles was found and Vlad drank it happily.

Then Paul took Vlad up to class where all the children were waiting with paints and paper.

'We are hoping that you'll pose for us so the children can paint you, and then we want to have a "*Vlad Week*" with pictures and stories about you all over the walls,' explained Mr Harris, the class teacher.

'What a wonderful idea,' agreed Vlad. 'Me all over the walls, I like that.'

'And on the ceiling,' said Mr Harris. 'We plan to have Vlad mobiles.'

Vlad's chest swelled out with pride and he grinned from ear to ear.

'Where do you want me to pose?' he asked.

'Right here, if you don't mind,' replied Mr Harris. 'Some of the children made this model castle – we tried to make it like Count Dracula's castle, so you'd feel at home.'

'It's a very good likeness,' said Vlad. 'Shall I stand on it?'

'Please,' said Mr Harris. 'And if you wouldn't mind dipping your hands into this red paint, then you really would look gruesome. Wonderful, that's right. Now let's see a really vampirish expression. Good, wonderful. Now off you go, children, let's see who can paint the most scary vampire.'

When the children had finished Vlad flew round and looked at their pictures.

'I look horrible,' he said contentedly. 'Just like Uncle Ghitza.'

Then the bell went for playtime.

'Out you go,' said Mr Harris. 'Come on, everybody out.'

'Can I go out and play too?' asked Vlad.

'Sure,' said Mr Harris.

Some of the children were playing Please Mr Crocodile.

'Let's play Please Mr Vampire,' suggested Vlad.

The children liked this idea.

'Please Mr Vampire,
May we cross your water,
To see your ugly daughter,
Just like you?'

'No you can't!' said Vlad, offended. 'I'm not ugly, and neither are my daughters.'

So the words were changed to:

'Please Mr Vampire,
May we cross your water,
To see your lovely daughter,
Just like you?'

'Only if you're wearing the colour green!' yelled Vlad, and all those not wearing green had to try to get past without being vampirized.

They all had a wonderful time and then some of the children wanted Vlad to go and play Dotball with them.

'Alright,' said Vlad. 'I'll be the umpire, the vampire umpire. Give me a whistle.'

Vlad flew up and down the football pitch blowing his whistle while the children picked sides and got into position.

'Okay you lot!' he shouted. 'Let's have a bit of law and order round here. Now anyone who argues with the ref gets vampirized, alright?'

'Alright,' agreed the children.

When Mr Harris came out to ring the bell for the end of play he was amazed.

'I've never been in such a civilized playground,' he said. 'You'll have to come to school more often, Vlad.'

'I should say so,' agreed Vlad. 'There's nothing like a vampire to put a bit of discipline into things.'

4

Vlad Goes Swimming

Judy and Paul were eating breakfast, Mum had gone to take her Saturday surgery and Dad was browsing through the newspaper.

'It's so hot,' complained Vlad. 'I can't stand it, us vampires come from a cold climate.'

'Well, fly around a bit,' said Judy helpfully. 'If you flap your wings enough, you should work up quite a breeze.'

So Vlad started flying about.

'It works!' he shouted. 'I feel quite cool, look at me!'

Vlad got so excited he didn't look where he was going and flew straight through Dad's paper. Dad was so surprised that he tipped off his chair backwards.

'What on earth are you doing?' he shouted at Vlad.

'Sorry,' said Vlad. 'I just wanted to cool down and then I got 'cited, you see.'

'I see,' said Dad, picking himself up. 'Well, it's only nine o'clock and you're in trouble already.'

'I'll take care of Vlad,' said Judy quickly. 'We're going swimming, we can take Vlad with us and he can cool down.'

'Swimming?' said Vlad. 'What's swimming?'

'It's what you do in the water,' Paul told him. 'Well, it's hard to explain. We'll go to the swimming pool and you'll see.'

So the three of them set off for the local pool.

'I'm not convinced this is a very good idea Judy, are you?' asked Paul on the way.

'No,' said Judy. 'Not at all sure, but we had to get Vlad out of the house, he's driving Dad crazy.'

'I didn't mean to fly through his newspaper,' explained Vlad. 'It was an accident.'

'Dad does get a bit bad tempered being at home every day,' said Paul. 'You can't blame him.'

'A bit bad tempered!' exclaimed Vlad. 'That's the understatement of the year. It's *don't* do this and *don't* do that. Gets on your nerves.'

'Alright Vlad, alright,' said Judy. 'You've made your point, now calm down and listen. The swimming pool will be full of people.'

'I'll vampirize them all,' said Vlad clacking his teeth.

'No you won't,' said Judy. 'You're going to be good. Now Vlad, you know people are still not used to you, so be sensible and don't scare anyone.'

'No one?' asked Vlad. 'Not even one teeny, weeny, little person?'

'No, not even one,' said Paul. 'Is that clear, or we're taking you home?'

'Oh alright,' groaned the vampire. 'Poor old Vlad, poor little Drac.'

Paul and Judy felt a bit anxious when they arrived at the pool and paid to go in. Vlad sat on Judy's shoulder while they went through the turnstile.

'What's that horrible smell?' he asked. 'Ugg, it's unbelievable! I don't think I like swimming pools.'

'Be quiet,' said Paul. 'All you can smell is the chlorine in the water. You'll get used to it.'

'People may get used to it,' announced Vlad, 'but a vampire, never.'

'Yes, you will,' said Judy. 'Now I'm going into the women's changing room. You go with Paul to the men's changing room.'

'No,' said Vlad defiantly. 'The men's changing room, never. It's the vampires' changing room or nothing for me.'

'It's not a problem, Judy,' Paul pointed out. 'Vlad doesn't have any swimming gear. He'll just have to watch.'

'Same old thing,' moaned Vlad. 'People have all the fun and the poor old vampire has to watch.'

A few minutes later the three of them were sitting together by the pool.

'Is that swimming?' asked Vlad. 'All those people splashing about?'

'Yes,' said Paul, 'and I'm going to join them.' He dived in and swam off across the pool.

'Watch where you're going!' yelled Vlad. 'You splashed me. You're not going in all that horrid smelling water too, are you, Judy?'

'It's alright, Vlad,' said Judy in a resigned tone. 'I won't go into the water until Paul comes out.'

So Paul and Judy took it in turns to look after Vlad. Gradually a small crowd gathered round them.

'Is that the vampire we saw on the telly?' asked one girl.

'Yeah,' said another. 'I saw his picture in the paper.'

'Can't vampires swim?' asked a third.

'Vampires swim very well,' replied Vlad. 'My Great Uncle Ghitza was a champion swimmer. Had I not left my swimming trunks at home in Romania, I could show all of you a thing or two.'

'You can sit on my rubber ring if you like,' said a

little girl. 'Look, I'll leave it there.'

Vlad flew on to the red ring where it floated in the middle of the pool.

'You see, vampires aren't afraid of the water!' he crowed.

For a while Vlad floated around greeting all the swimmers and threatening to vampirize anyone who splashed him, and to reinforce his scary image be sunk his fangs deep into the plastic ring. Within seconds Vlad and the ring began to disappear under water.

'Vampire overboard!' yelled Paul, trying madly to find Vlad.

Fortunately the swimming pool attendant had been watching and came rushing up with a huge fishing net to scoop Vlad out. A moment later Vlad lay on the side of the pool in a soggy little heap.

'What happened?' gasped the vampire.

'You vampirized your ring,' explained Judy. 'It was full of air, that's what kept you up.'

'Now she tells me,' groaned Vlad.

'We'd better take him home,' said Paul. 'He's dripping wet.'

So they took Vlad home and popped him in the tumble dryer.

Vlad waved as he went round.

'That was good,' said Vlad when the dryer had stopped. 'Can I have another go?'

'Not today,' said Judy.

'It's made me thirsty,' Vlad complained. 'What can I have?'

'Water?' suggested Paul.

'Ugg!' groaned the vampire. 'I nearly drank the whole swimming pool this morning. What else can I have?'

Paul opened the fridge. 'There's grapefruit juice, fizzy orange and milk,' he said.

'Boring,' moaned Vlad. 'What's that pink stuff up there?'

'That's for cleaning silver,' said Judy, taking it down off the shelf. 'Do you want to try some?'

'Please,' said the vampire, and soon the three of them were sitting, drinking and chatting happily.

'I think I ought to learn to swim,' said Vlad. 'You never know when it will come in useful. Show me what to do.'

'Alright,' said Paul. 'Look, you lie on your tummy. I'll lie on this stool – Judy, get Vlad a matchbox to lie on.'

A minute later Vlad was copying Paul. 'One, two, three, and a one, two, three,' they said together.

'Is that all you have to do?' asked Vlad.

'That's all,' said Paul. 'It's easy.'

Half an hour later Vlad had mastered doggy paddle and front crawl.

'What next,' he asked. 'This is too easy.'

'You could try butterfly,' suggested Judy.

'Uncle Ghitza would think that was rather soft,' said Vlad. 'How about bat stroke?'

A bit later, when Vlad had perfected this too (he said he was doing it right, and nobody argued), he climbed off the matchbox and yawned loudly.

'I'm exhausted. I think I'll go and have a little sleep in my drawer.'

The children were surprised.

'Well, it looks as if we're going to have an afternoon to ourselves,' said Judy. And they went outside to play.

At six they returned. Dad was preparing tea in the kitchen.

'Hello, Dad!' yelled Paul.

'I'm here,' called Dad from the kitchen. 'Is Vlad with you?'

'No,' said Judy. 'He had a bad experience at the swimming pool. So we taught him to swim when we got home. He said he was tired out and wanted a sleep.'

'A likely story,' said Dad. 'Well, I haven't heard a

peep out of him. Judy, you're filthy, go and have a bath before you come down to eat.'

'Must I?' Judy groaned.

'Yes,' said her father firmly.

Judy went upstairs and into the bathroom to run her bath. As she opened the door she heard the sound of splashing and, 'A one, two, three, and a one, two, three.'

'Hello, Judy!' shrieked Vlad. 'Look at me, I really can swim and dive.'

Vlad climbed up the chain that held the bath plug and dived into the full bath.

'Good, aren't I?' he said as he surfaced.

'Very,' said Judy. 'Now Vlad, you'll have to get out, Dad says I've got to have a bath.'

'Not in my private swimming pool,' said Vlad indignantly. 'A bath in my swimming pool, indeed. What a nerve!'

'Your private swimming pool?'

'Yes,' said Vlad. 'And since you're here, Judy, will you please go and get me the sun lamp and the inflatable cushion out of the car? Then I can sunbathe by my private swimming pool.'

Judy stared at Vlad dumbfounded.

'Don't just stand there gawping,' said Vlad impatiently. 'Go. and get my things, go on, move a leg, chop, chop.'

'But Vlad, Dad says I've got to have a bath.'

'You come any nearer my swimming pool and I'll splash you,' threatened Vlad, spraying Judy with water.

Judy decided to give up. She went downstairs to fetch the things Vlad wanted.

'Is that you, Judy?' called Dad.

'Yes,' said Judy, her heart sinking.

'Why aren't you in the bath?'

'I can't have a bath, Vlad's turned it into his private swimming pool and he splashes water everywhere if anyone comes near.'

'We'll soon see about that,' said Dad grimly, and he went to the cupboard and took out his raincoat and wellingtons.

'What are you going to do?' Judy asked.

'I,' said Dad, as he marched up the stairs, 'am going to liberate my bathroom and pull the plug out on Vlad.'

'You can't do that!' exclaimed Judy. 'He might go down the plughole.'

Dad flung open the bathroom door.

'Go away!' shrieked Vlad. 'This is my private swimming pool. You can't come in!' And he splashed vigorously.

Dad grabbed Vlad in one hand and pulled out the plug with the other.

'My swimming pool,' wept Vlad. 'I just learned how to swim and you've destroyed my swimming pool.'

'Well we do need, the bath, you know,' explained Dad.

'I don't see why,' said Vlad, sulking. 'Vampires don't have baths.'

'I've got an idea,' said Judy. 'We've still got that old rubber paddling pool, we can set it up in the garden and Vlad can swim and sunbathe there.'

'Sounds good,' said Vlad.

'You're on,' said Dad with relief. 'Now, Judy, bath!'

After the incident with the swimming pool, the children were always a bit worried when Vlad stayed at home with their father. One day, however, they came in and found Dad in a really good mood.

'I've had such a peaceful time,' he said. 'Vlad must have slept all day.'

'He's not in my drawer,' said Judy.

'Nor in mine,' said Paul.

'Well go and look for him,' said Dad. 'He must be around somewhere.'

The children searched and searched.

'We can't find him, Dad,' they reported. 'Where did you last see him?'

'Let's see,' said Dad. 'Yes, he was in the pocket of my raincoat when I went shopping.'

'He's probably still there,' said Judy.

'I hope not,' Dad gasped. 'I took the coat into the cleaners on my way home.'

The three of them dashed out, leapt into the car and drove straight to the dry cleaners. As they got out they could see Vlad through the window, sitting on the counter talking to the staff. They rushed in.

'Vlad, how can I ever apologize,' Dad burst out. 'I hope they found you in time.'

'In time for what?' asked Vlad. 'It was a treat, thank you so much. I really enjoyed myself. It was so nice and warm, even better than the tumble dryer. And that stuff they do the cleaning with is delicious. I was just getting the recipe from this gentleman here. And my clothes are *so* clean and I smell *so* delicious. Have a sniff.' And Vlad proudly held out an arm.

'You mean, you really enjoyed it?' asked Paul.

'Course,' said Vlad. 'Wasn't I meant to?'

5

Vlad's Concert

A few mornings later, after the children had gone to school and Mum had gone to work, Vlad was singing fretfully to himself as he watched Dad do the washing up.

> *'Vlad's got on the wrong side of Dad,*
> *It's very sad,*
> *It makes him feel bad,*
> *They'd better make it up*
> *They better had,*
> *It makes Vlad very sad,*
> *That he's not talking to Dad.'*

'What do I have to do to make you stop?' asked Dad.

'Talk to me.'

'I can't stop and talk now,' said Dad. 'I've got to practise.'

'I'll practise with you,' Vlad beamed. 'I'll play the piano, while you play the violin.'

Dad hesitated.

'Oh, well, alright,' he said. 'Come on then.'

So they went to the music room and practised together. In the middle of the morning Dad stopped for a cup of coffee and Vlad sampled some window cleaning fluid.

'Why aren't you working these days?' asked Vlad.

'No work,' said Dad gloomily. 'It's a bad patch.'

'I know how you feel,' said Vlad. 'No fun being unemployed.'

'What do you know about unemployment?' snapped Dad.

'What do I know about unemployment?' Vlad exclaimed. 'I sat under my stone for a hundred years with nothing to do. What's that if it's not unemployment? I bet you don't know anyone who's been unemployed for a hundred years!'

'Well no,' admitted Dad. 'Not yet.'

'Well then! People shouldn't go around making assumptions about vampires. Not know about unemployment, indeed!'

'Sorry, Vlad. I didn't mean to hurt your feelings.'

'That's alright,' said Vlad magnanimously. 'Anyway, I've just had an idea. Why don't we arrange to give a concert together? People will come just to see me, and then they'll all hear how good you are and you'll get lots of work.'

'That is a good idea,' agreed Dad.

So Vlad went and phoned his fan club and told them that he wanted to give a concert. The leader of the fan club thought it sounded a good idea too and went ahead with the arrangements. Soon there were advertisements in all the papers: 'Vlad the Drac, the famous vampire pianist, and Nicholas Stone on the violin, will be appearing together at the Carnival Hall.'

Vlad and Dad practised hard every day. The Carnival Hall soon told them that every seat had been sold and Vlad was very excited.

'It'll be good for the image of us vampires,' he explained. 'People will see our cultured side as well as our scary side.'

A few days before the concert Dad came into the music room to find Vlad sitting on the piano going through all the sheet music. The floor was littered with paper. Vlad was humming as he went through the music, chucking everything he didn't want on the floor.

'Stop it!' yelled Dad. 'What on earth are you doing?'

'Keep your hair on,' said Vlad cheerfully. 'I'm looking for a vampire song.' And he threw four more sheets of paper over his shoulder as he said it.

'Look at the mess you're making,' Dad exclaimed. 'The whole floor is, covered with paper.'

'It's alright,' replied Vlad. 'Judy can pick them up when she gets home – that's what girls are for.'

'No it is not!' shouted Dad. 'You just pick up all this paper yourself, this very minute.'

'Oh go jump in the river,' muttered Vlad.

'What did you say?'

'I said I'm sorry to put you to this bother.'

'That's not what it sounded like,' retorted Dad as Vlad flew round the room collecting the sheets of music and putting them in a neat pile on the piano.

'What's this, Vlad?' Dad asked, picking up a sheet Vlad had selected.

'It's my vampire song,' replied Vlad.

'Sweet Molly Malone isn't a vampire song,' said Dad, puzzled.

'It will be when I've finished with it,' said the vampire. 'You play the piano and I'll sing.'

So Vlad sang:

'In Dublin's fair city,
The girls are so pretty,
There once lived a fair maid,
Called Molly Malone,
She goes with her barrow,
Through streets wide and narrow,
Crying, cockles and mussels, alive, alive, oh!'

'I still don't see what it has to do with vampires,' said Dad. 'Just listen to my version,' Vlad chuckled.

'In London's fair city,
Where vampires are witty,
There once lived a vampire,
His name was Vlad the Drac.
He goes with his van,
Wherever he can,
Crying humans and people alive, alive oh!'

'That's jolly good,' said Dad, laughing.

'Join in the chorus,' called Vlad. So they both sang:

'Alive, alive, oh-ho,
Alive, alive, oh-ho,
Crying humans and people,
Alive, alive, oh!'

When it was over Dad clapped heartily. 'It's nice and scary,' he commented.

'Thanks,' said Vlad, glowing with pride. 'I'm glad you like it.'

As the day of the concert got nearer Vlad practised and practised. He explained to Judy that he had to be very fit as well as very musical.

'I do hope all those people will like my playing,'

he said. 'I've never played to an audience before, I'm jolly scared.'

'Don't worry, Vlad,' Judy reassured him. 'I'm sure they'll love you.'

'Better had,' said Vlad, 'or I'll vampirize them all!'

The night of the concert came and Vlad put on his bow tie. As the hall filled up he kept peeping through the curtains.

'Every seat's taken,' he whispered to Dad. 'It's going to be a full house.'

The curtain swept back and Dad and Vlad played and played. At the interval, however, the applause was polite but lukewarm. In the dressing room Vlad was in despair.

'My public don't love me,' he said, and covering his face with his hands he paced up and down the dressing table.

'I played as hard as I could,' he explained to the Stones. 'I raced up and down the piano, I leapt, I dived, I landed on all the right notes. What do those people want, blood?'

'Yes!' chorused the Stones.

'Uhhhh,' said Vlad and went and sat in a huddle with his back to them. Then he turned round and grinned.

'You mean those people want me to be vampirish?'

'No, not really,' said Mum quickly. 'Just pretend.'

'That gives me an idea,' said Vlad. And they went in for the second part of the concert.

Vlad stood on the grand piano, straightened his bow tie importantly, and held up his hand for silence.

'Ladies and gentlemen,' he announced. 'There are a few changes to tonight's programme. I, with the help of my good friend Nicholas Stone, am going to present you with a show never before seen by people, an evening of vampire folklore. To commence, my own version of that old Irish favourite, Sweet Molly Malone.'

So Vlad played and Dad sang as loud as he could.

'Everyone join in!' he yelled as they came to the chorus. And everyone did, singing with enthusiasm:

> *'Humans and people,*
> *Alive, alive, oh.'*

When it was all over at last the audience cheered and cheered. Vlad sat on Dad's head and smiled and blew kisses.

'Pick up your violin,' he whispered to Dad, while acknowledging the applause, 'and make scary noises in suitable places.' He stood up and turned to the audience. 'Ladies and gentlemen, I shall now recite a vampire poem for you, a lament for my Great Uncle Ghitza who was, as most of you know, very bad and wicked and who, after escaping from people many, many times, was finally killed by a telephone. Ladies and gentlemen, The Lament for Great Uncle Ghitza.'

Vlad cleared his throat.

'They went unto the castle grim,
That vampire for to find.
It really was the only thing
Those people had in mind.
The vampires gathered in a swarm
And went to Ghitza, him to warn.
Great Uncle Ghitza had a look,
And then he went and read a book.

They seek him here,
They seek him there,
Those people seek him everywhere.
Is he in hell or somewhere higher,
That damned elusive vampire?

It was a wild and windy night.
The men set out to find
The vampire whom they all declared

The worst one of his kind.'
'We'll have, no trouble finding him,
Those vampires really are quite dim.'
Great Uncle Ghitza had a peep,
And then he went and had a sleep.

The seek him here,
They seek him there,
Those people seek him everywhere.
Is he in hell or somewhere higher,
That damned elusive vampire?

They hurried to the tower dark,
They all declared, 'This is no lark,
That Ghitza he is somewhere here,
We'll not lose him, never fear.'
One cried, 'I'll never let him go,
Let's search for him both high and low.'
Great Uncle Ghitza had a sneer,
And then he wolfed a pint of beer.

They seek him here,
They seek him there,
Those people seek him everywhere.
Is he in hell or somewhere higher,
That damned elusive vampire?

They went unto the crypt down low,
Where lurked the spider and the crow.
They did not like it there one bit.
One said, 'Come, let's get out of it!'
Another cried, 'He must be here,
We cannot run away in fear.'
Great Uncle Ghitza took a glance,
Then went away and did a dance.

They seek him here,
They seek him there,
Those people seek him everywhere.

Is he in hell or somewhere higher,
That damned elusive vampire?

They went unto the castle spire.
(There was nowhere any higher.)
They said, 'He's gone and flown away,
We'll have to search another day.
These vampires are so hard to find,
You could go clean out of your mind.'
Great Uncle Ghitza had a laugh,
And then he went and had a bath.

They seek him here,
They seek him there,
Those people seek him everywhere.
Is he in hell or somewhere higher,
That damned elusive vampire?

The vampires danced with great delight,
Those dreadful men were in full flight.
Great Uncle Ghitza gave a yawn,
And then he went and mowed the lawn.

Little, little did they know
The vampire's days were numbered so.
He did not die by man alone,
His killer was a telephone.'

Dad played his vlolin creepily in the scary bits and the audience joined in the refrain.

When it was over, Vlad got a standing ovation. He flew into the auditorium and pretended to vampirize people, making everyone cheer louder than ever.

'For my last song,' said Vlad as he landed back on the stage, 'I am going to sing you a vampire Christmas carol, although it's out of season. I do hope you'll join in. The Twelve Days of Christmas,' Vlad whispered to Dad. So Dad played the introduction and Vlad cleared his throat, then he sang:

'On the first day of Christmas
Great Uncle Ghitza brought to me
A vampire up a gum tree.'

The audience laughed and laughed and Vlad went on till the end when everyone joined in again:

'On the twelfth day of Christmas
Great, Uncle Chitza brought to me
Twelve joggers jogging,
Eleven cyclists cycling,
Ten plumbers plumbing,
Nine drivers driving,
Eight boxers boxing,

Seven footballers footballing,
Six singers singing,
Five smelly socks,
Four rusty nails,
Three broken toys
Two chipped cups,
And a vampire up a gum tree,
And a vampire up a gum tree.'

The applause was thunderous and Vlad was gloriously happy. He was so exhausted by it all that he fell asleep in the car going home.

'It's not surprising,' said Mum. 'He's really worked very hard to make the concert such a success.'

So when they reached home Judy took the sleeping vampire out of the car very gently and crept upstairs to put him in his drawer.

'Goodnight little vampire,' she said fondly. 'Thank you for helping Dad.'

6

Vlad's Journey

One hot day shortly after Vlad had learned to swim Mum and Dad decided to take the children and Vlad to the sea as a treat.

'What's this sea thing?' asked Vlad.

'It's lots of water,' explained Paul.

'I *see*,' commented Vlad. 'Like a big bath, is it?'

'Well, no, not really,' said Paul, thinking hard. 'It's difficult to explain. Here, look at this map of the world. All this is land and all this here is sea.'

'Gosh!' said Vlad. 'There's a lot of it, isn't there?'

'There certainly is,' agreed Paul. 'Now, we are in London and here is the nearest sea at Brighton and this is where we're going.'

Vlad walked across the map and stood on London.

'If this is London, where's Romania?'

'It's here,' said Paul.

'Not far, really,' commented Vlad, walking over to Romania. 'How come I've travelled to England twice and never crossed the sea?'

'But you did,' said Paul. 'In the aeroplane.'

Next morning they all got up early, piled into the car and set off for the south coast. Vlad was bursting with excitement.

'Go faster!' he kept shouting at Mum, who was driving. 'Faster, can't you! Put your foot down, make it go faster. Overtake everyone, let's be the fastest car on the road!'

'Vlad, be quiet or you'll go in the boot,' said Dad firmly.

As they drove up to the motorway they saw a young man with long hair, a rucksack and a guitar, trying to thumb a lift. Mum drew up.

'Brighton any use to you?' she asked.

'Yes, great,' said the young hitch-hiker, and he climbed into the back of the car with Judy, Paul and Vlad. Vlad decided that he didn't like this stranger and sat on top of the rucksack glaring angrily at the young man.

'I don't see why we have to have him in the back seat with us,' he complained.

'There's plenty of room,' Dad pointed out. 'He needed a lift and we had space, it's a very sensible arrangement.'

'I don't think people should go travelling if they can't afford it,' said Vlad. 'Great Uncle Ghitza always said if you can't pay fly and if you can't fly stay at home. Great Uncle Ghitza had no time for hitch-hikers, none at all.'

'Vlad, stop talking nonsense,' snapped Dad. 'Great Uncle Ghitza didn't even know what a hitch-hiker was. You're making all of this up.'

'You could do with a haircut,' Vlad announced rudely to the hippie a moment later, 'to say nothing of a bath. Look at your hair, it's all over your shoulders . . .'

Eventually the young man got tired of Vlad.

'Give it a rest, you're a creep, man,' he said.

Vlad began to cry, and he howled and howled.

'Whatever did you say to Vlad to start this?' shouted Mum, drawing into a lay-by.

'All I said was you're a creep, man.'

'I don't think it was kind of you to call Vlad a creep,' said Judy.

'I don't mind him calling me a creep,' shrieked Vlad. 'But he called me *man* and I'm not a man, I'm a vampire!' and he continued to weep loudly.

'Gee, I'm sorry,' said the hippie. 'I didn't mean to hurt the little fella's feelings. You're a creep, vamp! Now, how's that?'

Vlad dried his eyes and beamed at the hippie. He held out his hand.

'That's fine,' he said. 'You're a creep, too, man.'

After that Vlad and the hippie were the best of friends.

As they drove on it began to get very hot in the car so they rolled down the windows. Vlad watched the cars go by. Then suddenly he leaned out of the window and started yelling: 'Road Hog! Why don't you learn to drive, four eyes! Idiot!' he shrieked at another car. 'That rusty lawnmower shouldn't be on the road.'

Judy grabbed Vlad but he was enjoying himself too much to be stopped, and he wriggled loose and shouted out of the other window: 'Women drivers are useless! We're the greatest!'

'Stop as soon as you can,' said Dad.

So Mum drew up, and another car stopped behind them. An angry man jumped out.

'Why do you think you're calling a road hog?' he shouted at Dad.

'It wasn't me,' expained Dad. 'I'm very sorry, it was our vampire.'

'You can't pull that one on me,' said the man. 'Come off it, a vampire indeed, I never heard such a silly story.'

'A silly story!' exclaimed Vlad, flying out and sitting on the man's shoulder. 'Just who do you think you're calling a silly story?'

'Get him off me!' yelled the man.

'Come here, Vlad,' said Judy sharply.

'He's got to say I'm not a silly story first,' said Vlad looking stern.

'You're not a silly story,' said the terrified man.

Satisfied, Vlad flew back to Judy.

'You really are a vampire, aren't you?' said the man.

'I most certainly am,' said Vlad, clacking his teeth in a menacing way.

'Don't worry,' said Dad. 'He's quite harmless. He's a vegetarian and wouldn't hurt a fly.'

'I've seen you on the telly,' said the man. 'Can I take your picture?'

'You most certainly can,' said Vlad. 'It's my pleasure. Give Dad the camera and I'll sit on your shoulder so we can both be in the picture.'

Dad took several photographs of the man with Vlad. They were the kind of photos that develop themselves on the spot, so Vlad was able to sign them for him.

'What's your name?' Vlad asked the man.

'Fred,' said the man.

So Vlad wrote: 'To Fred from Vlad.'

The man put his camera away and shook hands with the Stones.

'Pleased to meet you, no hard feelings I hope. My kids will be so thrilled to see these. Bye now.' And he drove off with the Stones, the hippie and Vlad waving him goodbye.

'Alright Vlad,' said Dad. 'Into the boot.'

'Why should I go into the boot?' asked Vlad indignantly. 'I didn't do anything. All I said was . . .'

'Yes, we all heard what you said. Now into the boot. If it goes on like this we'll never get to the sea.'

'I'm going to sponsify Dad,' grumbled Vlad to Judy, as Dad cleared out the boot.

'What does sponsify mean?' asked Judy.

'I don't know,' said Vlad. 'I just made it up – but whatever I decide it means, it's something nasty.'

'Do you often make up words?' Judy asked him.

'Not much else to do,' moaned Vlad. 'Poor old Vlad, poor little Drac, left on his own all the time. Anyway, why should vampires use people language? Hey Judy, listen to this word I made up. Rumbumbelow, rum-bum-bel-ow. Good, isn't it? Now you say it.'

'Rumbumbelow,' said Judy carefully.

'Hey, that's a good word,' said the hippie. 'I've never heard it before.'

'Not surprising,' Vlad told him. 'I just made it up.

It's a vampire word. I haven't decided what it means yet, I just like the sound of it – rurn-bum-bel-ow.'

'Boot ready!' called Dad.

'I'm going to sponsify you when we get to the sea,' muttered Vlad under his breath, and he climbed reluctantly into the boot.

Dad slammed it shut and walked round to the driving seat.

'You have a break, dear,' he said to his wife. 'That's better, now we can have a bit of peace.'

So they drove off happily. Dad began to sing and they all joined in. Then, in the distance, they heard the wail of police sirens.

'Nothing to do with us,' said Dad cheerfully, and went on singing until a police car overtook them and signalled for them to stop.

Dad got out of the car. 'What's the problem, officer?'

'That's the problem,' said the policeman, pointing at the boot.

The Stones listened. There were muffled shouts of 'Let me out, I'm suffocating' and kicks and bangs.

'Would you mind opening your boot, sir, and letting out whoever it is you've got in there?'

'You're not going to believe me,' said Dad.

'Try me,' said the policeman.

'It's not a person, it's a vampire.'

'I think you'd better let the poor devil out whoever it is.'

'Right you are,' said Dad and he unlocked the boot. To the Stones' surprise, Vlad was standing on the spare tyre looking perfectly calm and happy.

'Good morning, all,' he said and smiled broadly at everyone. 'No trouble, I hope?'

The policeman was confused.

'Well, it did rather sound as if you were locked up against your will,' he muttered.

'Oh no,' said Vlad. 'It's much nicer in the boot than being with all of those people in that stuffy old car – more privacy, you know.'

'Oh well, if that's the case,' said the policeman. 'I'm sorry I bothered you, sir.'

'Not at all,' said Dad with a smile.

As the policeman drove off Vlad glared at the Stones. 'I'll do that every time you put me in the boot,' he assured them.

'All right Vlad, you can sit in the car,' said Mum, 'on condition you promise never to shout at anyone again.'

'You've got yourself a deal,' said Vlad, climbing in. 'I'll sit on the shelf at the back and everyone will think I'm a lucky mascot.'

So Vlad sat quietly at the back muttering 'rum-bum-below, rumbum-bel-ow, rumbumbe-low' all the way to Brighton.

7

A Day by the Sea

When the Stones arrived at the seaside the horrors of the journey were quickly forgotten. They said goodbye to the hippie and went off for a walk along the front.

'He was nice,' said Vlad. 'I liked him after all. Funny thing about people, once you get to know them they often are quite nice. Maybe that's why Great Uncle Ghitza would never talk to people. No messing about with Great Uncle Ghitza – he just went straight in and – snap!'

Vlad flew on to Judy's shoulder and pretended to bite her neck. Other holiday makers on the promenade began to stare in amazement.

'It's the vampire we saw on TV,' said one.

'Isn't that the little fellow we read about in the papers?'

'That's Vlad the Drac!'

Vlad pretended to bite Judy again and then moved on to Mum.

A woman screamed and ran away. Vlad chuckled. 'I'm having a lovely time,' he announced. 'I'm scaring them all to death!'

'Stop it, Vlad,' snapped Mum. 'Everyone's looking at us.'

'I know,' said Vlad. 'That's why I like it.'

'Can we have some candy floss, please?' asked Paul.

So Dad bought four lots of the sticky pink stuff and handed them round. Vlad, sitting on Mum's shoulder, stared puzzled at the candyfloss.

'Whatever is it?' he asked, leaning over. And then headlong, he fell in.

Judy giggled. 'Vlad's been boiled, minced, frozen and liquidized; and now we've got a sugared vampire!'

The Stones watched in amazement as Vlad ate his way out of the candy floss. In a few moments there was none left, only a rather sticky Vlad with a broad smile on his face.

'That was nice,' he said appreciatively. 'I enjoyed that.'

'Come here, Vlad,' said Judy. 'I'll lick you clean.' So Vlad let Judy lick all the stickiness off him.

The Stones found a fairly empty spot on the beach and got into their bathing suits. Mum and Dad lay down to sunbathe and the children played in the sand.

Vlad decided that he liked the beach and helped Paul and Judy build castles and moats and canals. Soon half the children on the beach were wanting to join in, and Vlad was having a wonderful time telling everyone what to do. They built the most enormous sand castle anyone had ever seen. Vlad decided to make it just like Count Dracula's castle at home in Romania.

'Then,' he promised all the children, 'I will show you how I fly round the castle with my family.'

So the children worked very hard to build turrets and pointed roofs just as Vlad said. When it was finished Vlad announced that it was so authentic even Great Uncle Ghitza would be taken in and he did a demonstration flight on the dot of 2 pm. The children were delighted and clapped loudly.

'Come on, Vlad!' they called. 'Come and swim with us.'

So Vlad and the children went down to the sea.

'I can swim very well,' Vlad assured the children, but all the same he stayed on Paul's shoulder and looked rather doubtfully at the waves.

'Is that the sea?' he whispered in Paul's ear.

'That's right.'

'Well I don't like it!' muttered Vlad. 'It won't stay still, it's not a bit like the water in the bath. I don't want to go in the sea. You go on in. I'll sit and watch you.'

So Vlad sat on the wet sand looking suspiciously at the waves.

Suddenly one wave came a little further up the beach and drenched him. He shrieked and leapt up and ran away.

'I hate the sea,' he complained loudly to Paul. 'It keeps chasing me. Look! Did you see that, that nasty white stuff? It keeps chasing me.'

'That's only foam,' explained Paul. 'It isn't chasing you, it's the tide coming in.'

'Well whatever it is, I don't like it,' said Vlad and flew back to the sand castle.

'It's such a beautiful castle,' he commented, 'I really designed it well. I shall stand upon the ramparts of my castle and survey the horrible sea in safety.'

Vlad was so busy admiring his castle that he didn't notice the waves creeping nearer. Suddenly, he felt water lapping at his feet. He looked down and shrieked.

'Go back you horrible waves! Do as you're told. Get out of it. Judy, Paul, do something! Stop the sea destroying my castle.'

The two children dashed up.

'Come on Vlad,' said Paul. 'The tide comes in

twice a day, there's nothing anyone can do about it.'

'But what about my beautiful castle?' asked the distraught vampire. 'It'll get washed away.'

'That always happens to sand castles,' Judy explained. 'They're not meant to last, you can always build another one next time you're at the seaside.'

'You've got to be joking,' exclaimed Vlad.' 'Honestly, Judy, there are times when I think you are clean round the bend. Take me away. I never want to see that horrible sea again.'

Just then Mr Stone strolled up to see what all the fuss was about.

'Come on,' he said. 'Let's go and buy some ice-cream and see the Punch and Judy show.'

So they all went off to the pier. Vlad was still complaining.

'I don't like it here. The sea's all around us, and it's underneath as well.'

Vlad peered through the planks that made up the floor of the pier, moaning all the time, until they came to the Punch and Judy show. He stared, fascinated, at Mr Punch who was hitting everyone with his stick. Then Mr Punch picked up the baby.

'I'm going to throw this baby over the side,' Mr Punch told the children.

'Oh no you're not,' the children replied.

'Oh yes I am,' said Mr Punch.

'Oh no you're not,' they chorused.

Vlad burst into tears. 'The poor baby,' he wailed. 'I'll have to stop him,' and Vlad flew over to Mr Punch and grabbed his stick.

'Take that you brute,' yelled Vlad. 'And that and that and that!' And Vlad bashed Mr Punch on the head as hard as he could. The audience cheered delightedly. Then Mr Punch's wife came on.

'Thank you, Mr Vampire, thank you, thank you for saving my baby. Thank you for beating Mr Punch.'

'Who are you?' asked Vlad, puzzled.

'I'm Judy,' said the puppet.

'No you're not,' said Vlad. '*She's* Judy,' and he pointed to Judy Stone.

Mum came forward. 'They're both called Judy,' she explained.

'Oh,' said Vlad. 'Judy, meet Judy.'

'Hello,' said the puppet. 'Did you see what your vampire did to my husband? Isn't he wonderful! He saved my baby and he gave Mr Punch a hiding. Three cheers for Vlad, everyone.'

They all cheered loudly and Vlad beamed and bowed.

'Come on, Vlad,' said Dad, who felt that the situation might get out of control. 'We'd better be going.'

So Vlad sat on Dad's head and waved goodbye to all his admirers.

'Goodbye!' he yelled. 'Take care of the baby.'

As they left the Punch and Judy show behind Vlad grinned down proudly from his perch.

'I really showed that Mr Punch, didn't I?'

'You most certainly did,' the Stones agreed.

'I don't know about anyone else but I'm hungry,' said Paul.

'Me too,' said Judy.

'Let's go and have a hamburger,' suggested Mum.

'Good idea,' said Dad, so the family and Vlad went in search of a hamburger bar. They quickly found one and went in and ordered four king-size hamburgers.

Vlad looked at the hamburgers in disgust.

'They smell revolting,' he proclaimed. 'I don't know how you can eat them. Ugg, I feel sick, yuck.'

'Be quiet,' snapped Dad.

'What are they, anyway?' asked Vlad.

'Minced beef,' explained Judy.

'Well, if you'll believe that, you'll believe anything,' commented Vlad. 'Ugg, more like string and sawdust if you ask me.'

'Stop it, Vlad,' said Mum. 'You're putting everyone off their food.'

'Am I?' asked Vlad, cheering up. 'Jolly good! What's that big tomato doing in the middle of the table?'

'It's not a real tomato,' said Judy, giggling. 'It's plastic, it's full of . . .'

Dad put his hand over Judy's mouth, but it was too late.

'I know what it is!' shrieked Vlad, and he grabbed the ketchup container and flew all round the restaurant squeezing tomato sauce over everyone.

Eventually the manager caught him.

'Why did you stop me?' shouted Vlad, trying to escape. 'I was having so much fun. Let me go.'

'You just stop it,' yelled Dad dashing up. 'Look at all the mess you've made.'

'Oh dear,' said a contrite Vlad. 'Sorry, got 'cited you see.'

'I'm so sorry,' Dad apologized to the manager. 'We'll clear up all the mess.'

The Stones soon found themselves equipped with buckets of hot water and mops and cloths.

'What a way to spend a holiday,' complained Dad.

'You're a menace, Vlad, you really are,' said Mum.

'Yes, look what you've landed us in,' Paul moaned.

'You're all getting at me,' said Vlad. 'Poor old Vlad, poor little Drac.'

They were all working away when the hippie hitch-hiker wandered past the restaurant. He came

in to say hello, but when he heard what had happened he offered to stay and help. A few minutes later the Punch and Judy man popped in to have some lunch, and he offered to help out too. Several other people heard about the incident with the ketchup bottle and thought it was funny, and they also offered their services. So within an hour the whole place was returned to its normal state.

Vlad insisted on buying everyone a drink, including the manager, and persuaded them all to sing Sweet Molly Malone with him.

When it started to get dark, Mr and Mrs Stone said they really would have to be going home.

'Well,' said Dad as they got into the car, 'what a day, I feel a wreck but I must confess I did enjoy it.'

8

The Vampire's Revenge

One Thursday evening the Stones arranged to go and see some friends. When Vlad heard that only people were going to be there, he decided not to go.

'People,' he declared. 'I get bored with people, nothing but people. I'd rather stay home on my own and have vampirish thoughts.'

'Suit yourself,' said Dad.

So the Stones went off.

As soon as they returned, Judy dashed indoors.

'Hello, Vlad,' she called. 'We're back!'

There was no answer. Judy and Paul went from room to room calling, 'Vlad, we're home. Where are you?' But he was nowhere to be found.

'I expect he's just hiding to tease us,' said Mum.

'No, here's a note,' said Judy.

'What does it say?' asked Paul and Dad together.

Judy read: 'A vampire's got to do what a vampire's got to do.'

'Whatever does that mean?' said Mum.

'I hate to think,' commented Dad gloomily.

'Whatever it is, it'll probably be awful,' Paul agreed.

Dad sighed. 'I suppose we'd better phone the police.'

'Yes,' Mum nodded. 'That would be the best thing.'

Half an hour later a policeman arrived. 'I gather someone from your household is missing, sir,' he said to Mr Stone.

'Er – yes.'

'So who should I put on the missing persons list, sir?'

'Well,' said Dad, 'it's not really a person, officer.'

'Oh I see, sir. A pet, is it?'

'No, not exactly . . .'

'You will have your little joke, sir,' said the policeman, beginning to lose patience. 'Just who or what is missing?'

'Our vampire, officer,' said Mum.

The policeman stared at her. 'You do realize that the police are very busy people, madam, we don't have time to waste on silly jokes.'

'It's not a joke,' cried Judy. 'We really do have a vampire living with us, he's called Vlad the Drac, and we can't find him!'

'Just a minute,' said the policeman. 'That's the little fellow who plays the piano, isn't it? I've seen him on TV.'

'That's him,' said Judy.

'Well why didn't you say so in the first place?' And the policeman sat down and got out his notebook. 'Now, when did you last see the missing – er – vampire?' he asked Mr Stone.

'Earlier this evening. We all went out and left Vlad on his own. He didn't seem to mind, so we didn't bother with a vampire sitter, he said he'd watch TV and wash his hair.'

'Not many clues in that,' said the policeman. 'Well, I'll just have to check that they haven't heard anything at the station.' So he talked into his walkie-talkie. 'They don't know anything,' he reported to the Stones, 'except that all the telephones in this area are out of order, so you can't phone round.'

'It's very inconvenient,' said Mum, 'the telephones breaking down tonight of all nights.'

'I'm not sure that it *is* a coincidence,' commented Judy.

'Whatever do you mean?' asked the bewildered policeman.

'We passed the telephone exchange on our way to the swimming pool the other day. Vlad asked lots of questions about it and then got me to draw a map of the telephone exchange in relation to here.'

Paul groaned. 'I'm beginning to understand,' he said.

'That's more than I am,' said the policeman. 'Would one of you care to enlighten me?'

Judy took a deep breath. 'Well, you see, Vlad is very attached to the memory of his Great Uncle Ghitza. It appears that Great Uncle Ghitza was the wickedest of all the vampires. Even the other vampires were afraid of him. Anyway, Vlad says that Great Uncle Ghitza was killed by a telephone, and so Vlad has a thing about telephones.'

'How could a vampire be killed by a telephone?' asked the policeman in confusion.

'Vlad says he was strangled while trying to pull a phone out of the castle walls.'

'Oh,' said the policeman, looking even more confused.

'Well, we think Vlad may be trying to avenge Great Uncle Ghitza by attacking the telephone exchange.'

'That's what he must mean by this note "A vampire's got to do what a vampire's got to do",' added Paul.

'Are you suggesting,' asked the policeman, 'that your vampire may have something to do with this telephone exchange not working?'

'It looks rather like it,' said Dad gloomily.

'Come on,' said the policeman. 'Let's go!'

They all went out and piled into the police car and drove, sirens howling, to the telephone exchange. The car screeched to a halt and they leapt out. All the lights were on inside the building and there were sounds of music and laughter.

'They must be having a party in there,' said Mum. 'How very odd.'

The five of them went into the telephone exchange and up the stairs in the direction of the noise.

'They *are* having a party,' said Judy in amazement. 'And look, there's Vlad having the time of his life!'

And sure enough, there was Vlad, sitting with the telephone operators, knocking back the sherry and singing Humans and people, alive, alive oh.

'Hello!' he shouted when he saw the Stones. Come and join us. This is my new friend Louise.'

'Hello all,' said Louise. 'When the exchange went dead we didn't have anything to do, and the little fellow was so funny we decided to get out the Christmas sherry and have a party.'

'Vlad,' said Dad, shouting to be heard above the noise, 'are you responsible for this? The policeman here wants to ask you some questions.'

'The police?' said Vlad grinning broadly. 'Oh good! Good evening, Sergeant, guilty as charged. I did it to get a vampire's revenge for Great Uncle Ghitza. Have you got some hand-cuffs? No? What a pity! I was looking forward to being in the papers with handcuffs. Never mind, you can't have everything.'

'I think you'd better come down to the station with me, Mr – er – Vlad, and answer a few questions.'

'With pleasure,' said Vlad and he left the telephone exchange on the policeman's shoulder, waving to all his new friends as he went.

'Bye girls, carry on with the party. Don't forget to drink a toast to Great Uncle Ghitza.'

Down at the police station Vlad caused quite a stir. He told a group of reporters outside the police station: 'I did it for Great Uncle Ghitza. I vampirized the telephone exchange. The revenge of the vampire is swift and terrible.'

The cameras flashed as Vlad waved and shook his hands above his head.

'I did it!' he yelled. 'It was me, I did it!'

Eventually they managed to get Vlad inside.

It was decided to let him off with a caution on

condition be didn't try to avenge Great Uncle Ghitza again.

'It won't be necessary,' he assured them. 'I am content in the knowledge that Great Uncle Ghitza can now lie peacefully in his grave if he wants to. Let no one think, for one moment, that a vampire can be murdered with impunity. Let this be a lesson to everyone, young or old, male or female, black or white, that I, Vlad the Drac, will mercilessly avenge any vampire who . . .'

At that moment PC Wiggins put his helmet down over Vlad.

'Sorry about this, sir,' he said to Dad, 'but I had to stop him. He does go on a bit, doesn't he?'

'Vlad can go on for ever,' commented Paul.

PC Wiggins rapped on the helmet.

'Hello in there! If I let you out, do you promise to be quiet?'

'I promise!' yelled Vlad.

So the vampire was allowed out and he jumped into Judy's pocket, muttering furiously under his breath.

'Freedom of speech indeed, it's only for people not vampires. Poor old Vlad, poor little Drac.' And then, exhausted, he fell asleep.

9

Vladnapped!

The phone rang next morning as Mr Stone was practising his violin. Vlad picked it up.

'Vlad the Drac's residence, Vlad the Drac speaking.' Vlad glanced at Dad. 'Yes, he is here, but you don't want to talk to him – talk to me, I'm much more interesting.'

'Give me that,' said Dad.

'Patience, patience,' said Vlad and he returned to the phone.

'Sorry, I was rudely interrupted. What was that? Manchester, Newcastle, Birmingham and Glasgow – yes, that should be fine, hang about, I'll just ask him.' Vlad covered the receiver with his hand. 'It's a music agent, he wants us to do vampire concerts round Britain like we did at the Carnival Hall. Does that suit you?'

'Well – yes,' said a very surprised Dad.

'Good,' said Vlad and picked up the phone.' Yes, we'd love to do that. Go ahead and make all the arrangements. Thank you, goodbye.'

That evening Vlad, who was very pleased with

himself, sat on Judy's dressing table and watched her brush her hair.

'I'm pretty terrific,' he told Judy. 'I got Dad lots of work,' and he began to sing to himself in the mirror. 'Because I'm wonderful, that's what I am.'

'You've got the words wrong,' said Judy, 'it's because you're beautiful.'

'Because I'm beautiful,' sang the vampire.

'No,' explained Judy. 'You've missed the point. You don't sing it to yourself, you sing it to whoever you're with.'

'You mean I should sing "Because *you're* beautiful?"'

'That's right.'

'Oh, I couldn't do that,' said Vlad. 'I mean, I don't want to hurt your feelings, Judy, you're alright as people go, but I'm a vampire and I can only think vampires are beautiful.' And Vlad continued to sing to his reflection. 'Because I'm beautiful and wonderful and super splendiferous and the very cleverest vampire in the whole world.'

'I give up,' said Judy. 'You just won't behave like other people, will you?'

'I should most certainly hope not!' said Vlad in an outraged tone. 'Me behave like *people*? Never.'

A week later the Stones went to the railway station to see Dad and Vlad off. As the train left the station Vlad leaned out of the window.

'Bye,' he yelled waving frantically.

'Bye,' yelled Judy and Paul. 'Good luck!'

'Read about us in the papers,' Vlad called until he was too far away to be heard.

Every evening Dad phoned home with good news. The tour was going very well, they were playing to packed houses, and Vlad was enormously pleased with himself. Then late one night, when they were all in bed, the phone rang. Mum answered it sleepily.

'Hello darling,' she said. 'Why are you phoning so late?'

Judy and Paul clambered out of bed and stood in the hall listening.

'Oh dear,' said Mum. 'When did you find out that he'd gone? Yes I see, have you checked all the telephone exchanges? Oh, so he's not getting revenge again. Right, you go and fetch it, I'll hang on.' Mum turned to the children. 'Vlad's disappeared! Dad's just found a note on the floor. Yes, yes, what does it say? Oh no, £20,000. Who could ever imagine that we have that kind of money?'

'What does the note say?' asked Judy. 'Tell us.'

'It says: "If you ever want to see your vampire

again, leave £20,000 where we tell you within two days"'.

'Vlad's been kidnapped,' cried Judy bursting into tears. 'Whatever shall we do?'

'Phone if there's any news,' said Mum and put the receiver down. 'Keep calm, Judy, Dad's gone to the police, and he'll phone back if he hears anything.'

The Stones sat glumly in the kitchen drinking hot chocolate. When the phone went again Mum grabbed it instantly.

'Yes, yes,' she said. 'Alright, I'll tell the children, right we'll just have to sit and wait. Better try and get some sleep now. Good night darling, try not to worry too much.' She put down the phone. 'Dad says the police don't think it's hardened criminals, but to be on the safe side not to say anything to the newspapers and TV, because sometimes that makes the kidnappers desperate.'

'Vlad won't like that,' said Paul. 'Something is happening to him and there'll be nothing about it in the papers.'

'Well, it's for his own good,' said Mum.

The next morning Paul picked up the newspaper from the mat and was amazed to see the headline: 'Mysterious Disappearance of the Musical Vampire – Where is Vlad?' He rushed into the kitchen to show the paper to the others.

'Look at that,' he said.

'It's very odd,' said his mother. 'If *we* didn't tell the papers and neither did the police, *who* did? It must have been the kidnappers, I suppose. How odd.'

All that day Judy and Paul sat through school quite unable to concentrate. They rushed home at four o'clock but there was still no news. Mum made some supper but no one felt like eating. Then the phone rang. It was Dad, but there were no developments.

'You might as well put the television on,' said Mum. 'No point in just moping around.'

When the news began the Stones sat up in amazement. The newsreader said, 'We have just received a call from some people who claim to be holding Vlad the Drac to ransom. The caller said, "Vlad is alive and well. Save the vampire before it is too late." Earlier today we received a note with blood stains on it which states, "This is vampire's blood. If you want to save the noble Vlad, act now".'

'At least he's still alive,' said Judy. 'What a relief!'

'I just can't understand who contacted the newspapers and TV,' Mum said.

'Anyway, he's getting lots of publicity,' said Judy. 'Poor little thing, he's probably locked away somewhere awful and doesn't know what's happening.'

'Poor Vlad,' agreed Paul.

The next day there were more Vlad headlines in the newspapers: 'The Vampire Lives, but for How Long?' And Judy got a letter in strange handwriting. She ripped it open and inside was a piece of Vlad's coat with a note saying: 'This is cut from your vampire's coat. Save the rest of him by paying up quick.'

Judy burst into tears. 'Poor Vlad. Poor, poor little Vlad, all he wanted was to improve vampire-people relations, and *this* happens to him. What will he think of people now? What can we do to help? We can't just sit here.'

'Where does the letter come from?' asked Paul.

Mum looked at the envelope. 'It's from Scotland,' she said. 'Get an atlas, I'll look the place up. Yes, look here it is, it's a tiny place in the north of Scotland.'

'Let's go and look for him,' said Judy. 'We must go, before it's too late.'

'I can't see what good we can do,' said her mother, 'but it would be better than just sitting here. Go and pack a few things. I'll ring the surgery and tell them I'll have to take a few days off, then we'll ring Dad and tell him to meet us.'

That night the Stones were installed in a hotel in the village from which the letter came.

'Let's see if there's any news of Vlad,' said Dad, turning on the television. They waited eagerly for the news. At last it came:

'Despite threatening phone calls to every newspaper and TV station in the country, the mystery of the missing vampire continues. Fear for the safety of Vlad the Drac mounts with every day of his continuing ordeal.'

Much later Judy lay in bed, unable to sleep with worry about Vlad. She tossed and turned. Suddenly, she heard something fall on to the floor. She got up and put on the light. Lying on the floor was a note.

'Come and fetch your vampire – you'll find him in the ruins of the castle. Tell no one if you value the vampire's life.'

Judy flung on her clothes and crept into Paul's room. She shook him awake.

'Come on,' she whispered urgently. 'I've got a note to fetch Vlad. I'll meet you outside in five minutes. Bring the torch.'

So a few minutes later the children crept out and began to climb up the hill to the ruined castle.

'Poor Vlad,' said Judy. 'Do you think we'll get there in time?'

'Don't waste breath talking,' answered Paul. 'Come on, let's run.'

After a long, rough and chilly climb, the children reached the castle. It loomed grey and grim in the darkness. The silence was eerie, and the moon shining down on the ruins made it look strange and frightening.

'I'm scared,' said Judy.

'Me too,' said Paul. 'Hold my hand. Come on, we must try to find Vlad.' Paul shone his torch on the walls that surrounded him. 'He's around somewhere,' he said. 'Look.'

Judy looked up and saw written on the wall VAMPIRES RULE OK? and GHITZA IS THE GREATEST, VLAD FOR KING. Then out of the night came a piercing shriek. Judy and Paul clung together.

'What was that?' gasped Paul. Then they heard the rattling of chains and another blood curdling scream.

'Vlad, Vlad where are you?' called Judy.

'Vlad, we've come to, rescue you!' shouted Paul. They listened hard, terrified, in the silence, then suddenly a white spook flew over them shrieking and howling.

Judy crouched down and covered her head with her hands. She screamed, 'Make it go away Paul, make it go away!'

Paul flapped at the spook but remorselessly it dived down on to Judy's shoulder.

'Hello,' said the spook. 'I fooled you, I fooled you! It's all right, it's only me having a bit of fun pretending to be the ghost of Great Uncle Ghitza. Judy, it's only Vlad, I'm here under this tissue.'

Judy stopped screaming and peered round, and there was Vlad looking as fit as a fiddle and very pleased with himself.

'I really scared you, didn't I?' he said, grinning broadly.

'Oh Vlad,' said Judy. 'How could you do such an awful thing, you nearly scared me to death.'

'I know,' said Vlad. 'I'm such a naughty little vampire. Come and meet my friends, they're hiding down in the dungeon.'

'Your friends?' said Paul. 'But we thought you were kidnapped.'

'Well I was, sort of,' said Vlad. 'I was Vladnapped. After a few hours they wanted to let me go, but I was having such a good time.'

The children followed Vlad down to the dungeon. There sat a teenage couple looking white and exhausted. The girl burst into tears.

'Take him away, please take him away. Look, here's two pounds, it's all we've got, but you have it and take him away.'

'These are my friends, Rob and Marie,' Vlad announced. 'They only Vladnapped me because they want to start a restoration fund for this lovely old castle. Jolly good idea, I reckon – wouldn't mind this place as a holiday home myself!'

'We don't want the money,' wept the girl.

'No,' said Rob. 'And I'm beginning to think we don't even want the castle either. Right now, we just want to get away from *him*. We haven't slept for three days or nights, he hasn't stopped talking.'

'Yes,' said Vlad. 'I told them all about Great Uncle Ghitza. I knew they'd be interested, seeing they're so keen on castles.'

'One thing I don't understand,' said Paul to the Vladnappers, 'is why did you two send all those letters and make all those phone calls? They must have cost you a fortune.'

'We didn't do any of it,' said Rob. 'He did.'

'Vlad!' exclaimed Judy. 'Why did you do that? We've been so worried.'

'I was just having a bit of fun,' explained Vlad. 'I liked being in the newspapers every day and on TV. Even my concerts didn't attract that much attention.'

'You won't call the police, will you?' begged the girl. 'We offered to set him free the day we took him but when he got to know about the castle he just wouldn't go. He insisted we bring him up here, and he's been telling us his horrible, creepy stories ever since. It's so cold and I'm so scared!' And she started to sob again.

'I like this castle,' explained Vlad. 'And when it's been cleaned up a bit it'll be a marvellous haunt for vampires as well as ghosts.' Then he was off again, flying round the castle in his white tissue, shrieking and howling.

Paul caught him as he swooped. 'Now you stop that. We've all had a terrible few days because of you. We're going to the hotel to tell Mum and Dad that you're safe and then they'll have to tell the police to stop the search.'

'Yes,' said Judy as she turned to Rob and Marie. 'You two had better go. We won't tell on you, he's obviously given you a pretty rough time.' They staggered off thankfully. 'And as for you, Vlad, if I wasn't so pleased to see you, I'd be very, very angry.'

'I don't see why,' complained Vlad, 'I haven't done anything. I couldn't help being Vladnapped! Poor old Vlad, poor little Drac.'

10

Vlad Makes Good

When Vlad and the children got back to the hotel, they woke Mum and Dad and told them the good news. Vlad had been found and was safe and sound.

When the whole story was out Mr Stone was furious.

'How could you do such a thing?' he yelled at Vlad. 'We've been worried sick. Mum's taken time off from work, Judy and Paul have missed school, it cost a lot of money for us to come up to Scotland and stay in this hotel, and half the police in Britain are looking for you. All because you wanted to play silly jokes. I hope you're good and ashamed of yourself.'

'Sorry,' muttered the vampire, looking at his feet. 'Didn't mean to be bad.'

'I suppose it all seemed very funny to you, sending gruesome messages to the TV and the newspapers, and letters to Judy that made her cry. Now I'll have to ring the police. What I'm going to say to them I do not know.'

'Calm down, darling,' said his wife. '*I'll* phone the police.'

'Well, whichever one of us phones them is going to feel a fool. Alright, you go and phone. I haven't finished with this vampire yet. I am sick and tired of having our life disrupted by you, Vlad. The first thing I'm going to do when I get back to London is book your flight home to Romania.'

'What about the film première?' asked Judy.

'Oh alright, he can stay for that, but the very next day – back to Romania he goes, and that's that. And until you go back to Romania, Vlad, you will stay quietly in your drawer and not go out and not annoy anyone and not play any tricks. I just don't want to know you're there. Is that clear?'

'Yes,' said the crestfallen vampire.

'Good,' said Dad. 'Now I'm going back to bed. I suggest you do the same.' And with that he stomped out of the room.

The next day the family went home on the train. Vlad was still very quiet.

'You just remember, you're not popular around here,' Dad reminded him. 'And I don't want one single, solitary squeak out of you. Understand?'

Vlad nodded miserably. 'Do you think it might amuse Dad to see my vampire ghost act?' he whispered to Judy.

'No,' said Judy. 'I don't really think it would, Vlad. Just be very quiet. Dad's very angry.'

'I'll make it up to him, you'll see,' said Vlad.

'I think it would be better if you didn't do anything else at all,' Judy told him.

'Wish I didn't have to go to this rotten old first-night,' said the vampire with a miserable sigh. 'Wish I could go straight back to Mrs Vlad and the children.'

Vlad was very quiet for a few days afterwards, too. Then one morning a Rolls Royce drew up outside the house and a uniformed chauffeur knocked at the door.

'Car for Mr Vlad the Drac,' said the chauffeur.

'Vlad,' said Mum suspiciously, 'what's all this about?'

'It's a secret,' said Vlad. 'I can't tell you.'

'Promise it's nothing bad?'

'Vampire's honour,' promised Vlad. 'Cross my heart and hope to die.'

'I'm not sure I'm doing the right thing,' said Mum as she let him go.

'You are, really you are,' Vlad assured her. 'And remember: it's a secret. Don't tell anyone.'

Every day for a week the car came for Vlad. If

Dad was at home the car would park round the corner and Vlad would slip out by the back door.

'I wonder what Vlad's up to,' Judy mused to her mother.

'I don't even want to think about it,' said Mum. 'If he gets into any more scrapes Dad will blow the roof off the house!'

However, all seemed to be well. So the evening before his return to Romania Dad said Vlad could come down and join them for supper. Vlad was in good form as the first night of *The Wickedest Vampire in the World* had been a big success and anyway he was looking forward to going home. After supper Vlad asked if he might demonstrate his acrobatics on the mobile hanging from the ceiling.

'Well, yes, you can,' said Mum, 'but let's just get these dishes cleared away first so there isn't an accident.'

Dad and the children helped clear the table and Vlad got ready to perform. He flew up and caught hold of the mobile and swung backwards and forwards, singing at the top of his voice.

'He flies through the air
With the greatest of ease,
That daring young Vlad
On the flying trapeze.'

When the performance was over the family applauded politely. Dad looked at his watch.

'It's Vlad's last night and it's two hours to the children's bedtime. What shall we do?'

'Watch TV,' said Vlad.

'Wouldn't you rather talk to us?' asked Judy disappointedly.

'No,' insisted Vlad. 'I want us all to watch TV together.'

So the Stones sat round the TV and Judy turned it on.

'It's the wrong programme,' complained Vlad. 'How can I change over?'

'You press this,' said Mum, showing him the hand control set. 'Look.'

Vlad was fascinated. 'Let me do it,' he said. 'Put it down there,' and Vlad began to dance on the controls.

'Look at me!' he yelled as the different programmes flashed up on to the screen one after another. 'I'm the champion vampire zapper!'

Dad grabbed Vlad. 'Now stop that,' he said, trying not to get angry. 'What is it you want to watch?'

'Sorry,' said Viad. 'Got 'cited, you see.'

'Now then. Let's see. Yes, press the button marked 3.'

They just caught the end of a comedy show and then came the commercials. Vlad was in all of them!

The first was for washing-up liquid. It showed Vlad snatching a bottle of washing-up liquid from a surprised looking woman and saying, 'Don't wash up with my supper, what a waste,' then drinking it and saying, 'It's kind to my throat. It'll be kind to your hands.'

Next came a furniture polish advert. Vlad was sitting on a highly polished wooden table. 'Use the polish that vampires take a shine to,' he beamed at them from the TV screen.

The last commercial was about shoe polish. Vlad was sitting on the floor with lots of children in brightly coloured shoes dancing round him. He sang:

'Yellow, orange, green and blue,
Shoes of many a bright hue,
Polish makes your shoes look good.
Vlad the Drac thinks that you should
Polish them once a day,
So that everyone will say:
Shoes polished with vampire food,
Do indeed look very good.'

When the commercials were over, the Stones sat in stunned silence.

'What's the matter with you lot?' asked Vlad. 'Cat got your tongue? Now that's what I call a really good evening's viewing.'

'Is that where you went in your car each day, to make commercials?' asked Mum.

'That's right, and I made lots and lots of money. So now I'm going to make it up to Dad, like I promised.'

'Oh dear,' said Dad. 'What now, I wonder?'

'May I present you with this envelope, with greetings and thanks from the vampires of the world, who unite in giving thanks to you and have unanimously decided to make you the director of The Great Uncle Ghitza Memorial Fund for Unemployed Musicians.'

'What on earth's that?' said Dad, looking confused.

'I've given most of the money I earned to a fund for unemployed musicians, to make up for being so bad. Will you be my friend again?'

'I don't know what to say,' gasped Dad. 'This is truly wonderful. There are so many people it will help.'

'It's great, Vlad,' enthused Paul. 'Simply brill.'

'You're wonderful, Vlad,' Judy added, patting him on the head.

'We'll have to let by-gones be by-gones now,' said Mum. 'It really is very generous of you.'

'Let's drink a toast to Vlad,' suggested Dad, and he poured out five drinks. 'Let us raise our glasses to Vlad the Drac, and wish him a happy reunion with his family, and may he return to England soon . . . Well, not too soon. To Vlad and to Great Uncle Ghitza and Absent Vampires wherever they may be.'

'Vlad, Great Uncle Ghitza and Absent Vampires!' said Mum, Judy and Paul, raising their glasses.

'Speech, speech,' called the family.

Vlad cleared his throat. 'Ladies, gentlemen and children, unaccustomed as I am to public speaking, I feel I must respond to the generous and heartfelt toast just made by Dad. On behalf of Great Uncle Ghitza (who would vampirize you all on the spot if he were here) and vampires everywhere, I want to thank all you lovely people who have been so kind to me while I've been staying in your wonderful country, and on the eve of my return to Romania I want you all to know there is a bit of my heart that I will leave behind in London. Is that enough, or do you want me to go on?'

'No, no,' said Mum quickly. 'That's fine, Vlad, very nice indeed.'

Later that night when Judy was trying to get to sleep she felt Vlad nibbling her ear. She sat up, yawning.

'Oh Vlad, what is it, I was just about to nod off.'

'Well, you'll just have to wake up,' said the vampire firmly. 'I've got something important to tell you. It's a secret no one is going to know about but you and me.'

'Is it a nice secret?' asked Judy suspiciously.

'I think so,' said Vlad. 'Do you remember Rob and Marie, the young pair that vladnapped me? Well, they only did it 'cos they wanted to save that lovely old castle. And I thought it'd be such a nice place to bring Mrs Vlad and the kids to visit that I've got some money for them to start the fund with. Here's their address, you take them the money.'

'That is very, very nice of you, Vlad,' said Judy.

'I know,' grinned the vampire. 'If you ever meet my Great Uncle Ghitza, don't tell him! Although,' he added, grinning even more broadly, 'in the circumstances I think Great Uncle Ghitza might be rather proud of me.'

The next day the Stones drove Vlad to the airport.

'I'm really looking forward to going home,' commented Vlad as they walked across the car park. 'The visitors to the castle must have been missing me terribly.'

'Vlad,' called Dad who had gone on ahead. 'You're wanted in the VIP lounge before you get on the plane.'

'VIP lounge?' said Vlad. 'What's that?'

'It stands for Very Important People,' explained Paul.

Vlad sat down. 'I'm not going in there,' he announced. 'I want a VIV lounge for Very Important Vampires.'

Mum thought quickly. 'Paul got it a bit wrong,

Vlad. VIP stands for Vampires and Important People.'

'Oh well, that's all right then,' said Vlad, and he flew off happily.

A moment later he swooped back to the Stones in great excitement.

'That Vampires and Important People lounge is full of people who've come to see me. They've all come to see *me* off!'

Sure enough, in the airport lounge were Vlad's entire fan club with banners saying 'Come back soon Vlad' and 'Long live the Vampire', and Judy's class from school with Mrs Thompson, PC Wiggins, the Punch and Judy man, in fact everyone Vlad knew. Vlad was delighted and flew round talking to everyone.

After a while he flew over to Judy. 'What do you think of that?' he asked. 'All the people have come just to see me. You know, people aren't so bad after all.'

Judy felt a tap on her shoulder and turned round. It was Rob and Marie!

'We had to come,' said the girl. 'We got the money and we knew it was from you. We're going to join your fan club and tell everyone vampires are the greatest.'

Vlad grinned. 'It was for the castle,' he said. 'And mind you're good from now on or I'll be back to vampirize you.'

'Flight 709 to Romania boarding now, will all passengers for flight 709 to Romania board now.'

'That's my plane,' yelled Vlad. 'Bye every-one, I'll come back soon - but not too soon. Rumbum-below!'

And a few minutes later they were all waving to the plane as it disappeared into the clouds taking the vampire home to his castle.

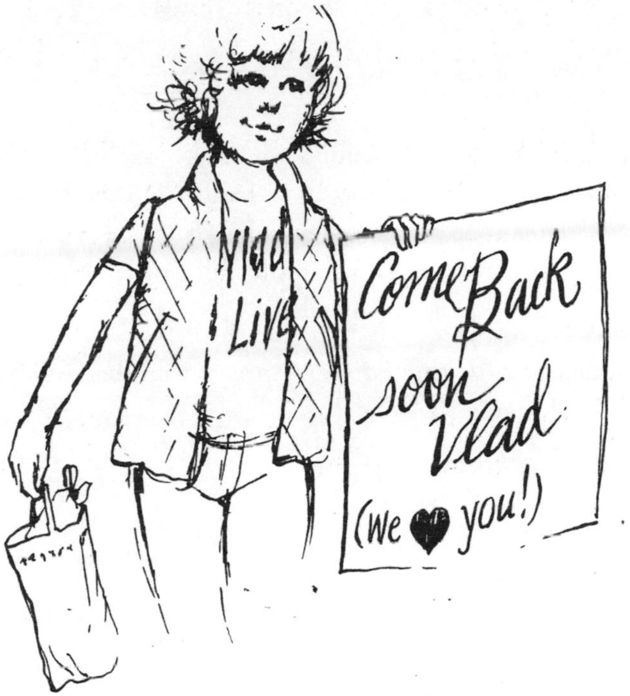

Vlad Live
Come Back soon Vlad
(We ♥ you!)

About the Author

Ann Jungman lives in London where she was born. After training as a lawyer Ann began to teach and then to write. Ann is the author of more than a hundred books for children, ranging from picture books to full length novels. Part of each year is spent in Australia.

In addition to writing books, Ann is a publisher and runs Barn Owl Books.

IF YOU ENJOYED *Vlad the Drac Returns* YOU MIGHT LIKE TO READ THESE OTHER BARN OWLS:

VLAD THE DRAC

by Ann Jungman

ISBN 1-903015-22-7 £4.99

This is the first book about Vlad the Drac.

When Judy and Paul get talked into bringing a tiny vampire from Romania to England, they have no idea of the trouble they are storing up. Vlad may be a vegetarian and harmless but he does like to wander around the house and can't resist pretending to be a scary bloodsucker. How long can Judy and Paul keep him a secret?

"These stories are excellent for young readers" Nicholas Tucker in *The Rough Guide to Children's Books*

YOU'RE THINKING ABOUT DOUGHNUTS

by Michael Rosen

ISBN 1-903015-03-0 £4.99

It was COLD, spooky and very boring.
Frank hated Friday nights, sitting in a museum, while his mum did the cleaning. He felt very alone . . . until a skeleton came over for a chat.
"How about a doughnut?" asked the skeleton.
"O.K." said Frank.
And suddenly the museum didn't seem quite so boring any more.
After a few chilling encounters with some of the skeleton's weird and wonderful friends, all Frank really wants is his mum . . .

Spooky fun from poet Michael Rosen

THE AMAZING ADVENTURES OF GIRL WONDER

by Malorie Blackman

ISBN 1-903015-27-8 £3.99

Girl Wonder is Maxine and being the oldest, of course, she is the one who has to solve all the problems. The twins Edward and Anthony, being younger, are always suspicious of their big sister's schemes but usually go along with them. The results are often disastrous and always hilarious.

Malorie Blackman has chosen the very best from the three Girl Wonder volumes to create a new book full of the author's favourite heart-warming stories.

"Sparkling Stories" *Children's Books of the Year*

THE MUSTANG MACHINE

by Chris Powling

ISBN 1-903015-06-5 £3.99

The Mustang Machine is a magical bike, whoever owns it will be faster than anyone else. That makes it absolutely vital that the machines does not fall into the wrong hands. One way or another Tim and his friends have to find a way to stop Dennis Doggerty, the local bully, claiming the bike as his own.

A moving funny story about a group of kids, an old man and a magic bike winning through and winning through fairly . . .